How to use this bo

Relax and enjoy!

Kumon's Step-by-Step Stickers are designed so that children and parents can learn and have fun together. Children learn best from active and participatory parents, so please help your child with the activities in this book. By helping, you are encouraging your child to develop a love of learning, and laying the foundation for him or her to become a self-motivated learner.

 To make the exercises easier for your child, please cut out the illustrated portion of each page for him or her.

 At the beginning of this book, your child will practice pasting stickers anywhere he or she likes on the illustrated portion of each page. It may be a good idea to peel off the appropriate stickers for each page for your child. Or if your child can peel off stickers well, you can remove each sheet of stickers and give each sheet to your child as he or she progresses through the book.

 When your child has completed each page, please offer him or her lots of praise.

 Please refer to the "To parents" notes in this book, which provide more comments and advice on how to help your child enjoy and learn from this book.

 Try to limit the number of pages your child will complete in a day. It is best to end the day's work when your child still wants to do more.

Tips

● If your child is using stickers for the first time, it may be a good idea to peel off the appropriate stickers for each page and hand them to your child. Children enjoy the tactile experience of peeling stickers, too; if your child would like to try peeling stickers independently, encourage him or her to peel the stickers off slowly and carefully so that the stickers do not tear. When he or she has done so, offer lots of praise.

● Before your child begins, ask him or her to choose a place on the page to paste the sticker. Next, encourage your child to carefully hold the edge of the sticker and place it down on the paper. This is difficult for young children, so please hold the paper steady for your child at first. Then ask your child to use his or her fingers to flatten the sticker on the designated area so it is smooth.

● Your child may already be familiar with playing with stickers, but perhaps he or she is used to just pasting them randomly. It may be difficult at first for your child to place stickers onto a specific place, but be patient. In time, your child will master this skill.

This child is holding the edge of a sticker and attempting to stick it onto the designated place.

It does not matter if your child cannot sticker accurately or if the image he or she has created is not perfect. Your child will gradually learn how to align the edges.

Time for Takeoff

To parents

Please remove the first sheet of stickers and give it to your child. (This sheet of stickers is for exercises 1 through 3.) Up until exercise 6, your child will freely paste stickers onto a background. When he or she is finished, please offer lots of praise and say "airport" aloud while pointing to the word.

Paste the stickers as you like.

airport

Hard at Work

Example

To parents

Please encourage your child to peel each sticker off slowly and carefully so that it will not tear. Peeling off and pasting tiny stickers is not an easy skill for young children to learn. Your child must gain the ability to control the fine movements of his or her fingers. When your child is finished, please offer lots of praise.

Paste the stickers as you like.

construction site

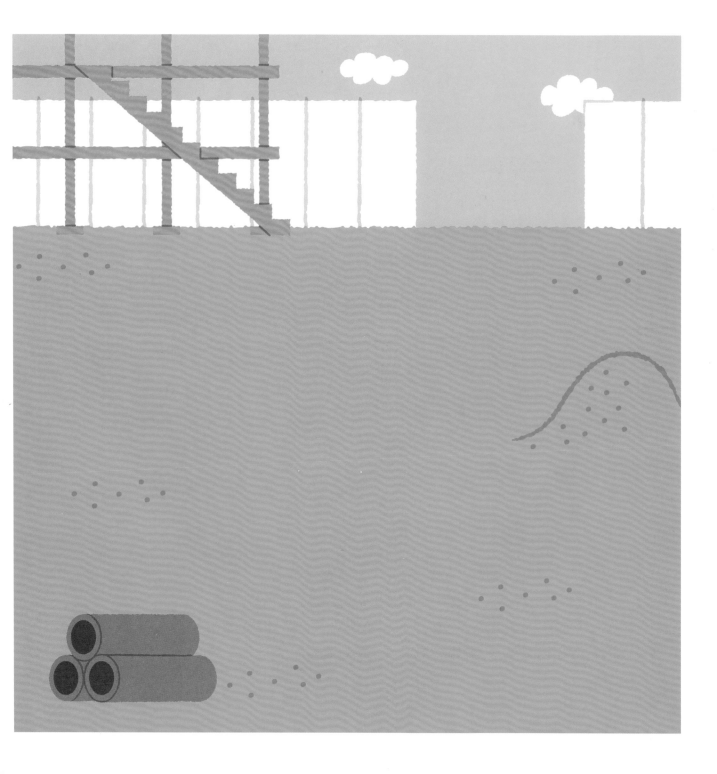

Let's Go!

To parents

When your child is finished, talk with him or her about the picture. You can say something like, "This is a bus, and this is a taxi. What is this?" or say "train station" aloud while pointing to the words. Your child will be more and more interested in letters and words.

Paste the stickers as you like.

train station

Board the Bus

Example

Paste the stickers as you like.

bus stop

 # On the Road

 Example

Paste the stickers as you like.

road

6 Paddle around the Pond

To parents

The stickers will become smaller and smaller as your child progresses through the workbook. It is not easy for young children to learn to peel off and paste tiny stickers. When your child is finished, offer lots of praise.

Paste the stickers as you like.

pond

7 Garbage on the Go

Paste the sticker onto the garbage truck.

garbage truck

Concrete Cab

To parents

The sticker for this page is round, too. The white circle is a little smaller than the sticker to make it easier for your child to cover the white space. It does not matter if your child cannot paste the sticker perfectly on the white area. He or she will gradually learn to paste more accurately.

Paste the sticker onto the cement truck.

cement truck

Express Route

To parents

In this exercise, your child will practice aligning the edges of the sticker with the white space. When your child is finished, talk about the picture together. You can say, "Express trains only stop a few times so they are faster than local trains that stop a lot," or "express train" aloud while pointing to the words.

Paste the sticker onto the express train.

express train

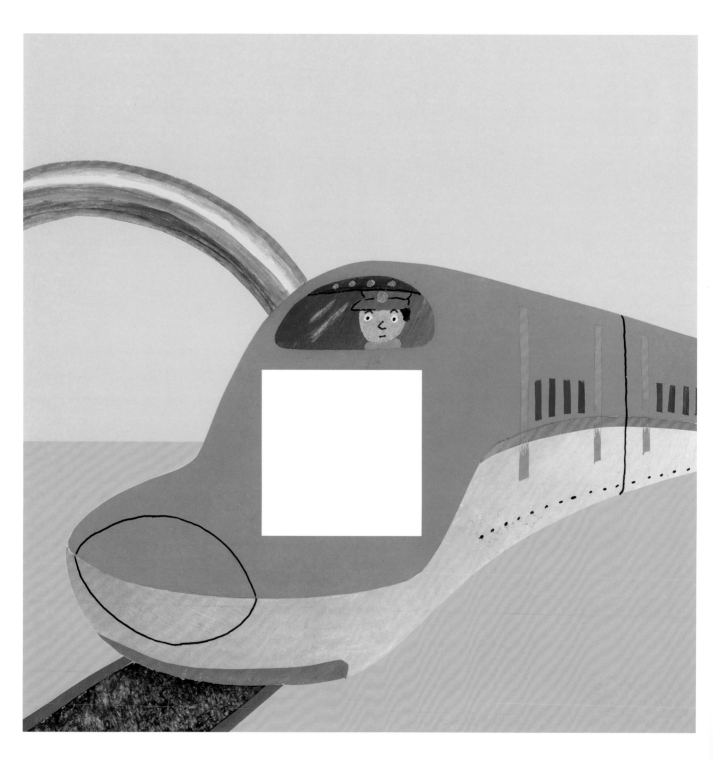

To the Rescue

To parents
This exercise is a little more difficult because the sticker is rectangular and your child must match the sticker's orientation to the white space. Please offer lots of praise if he or she can align the edges. It does not matter if your child cannot paste the sticker perfectly on the white area.

Paste the sticker onto the fire engine.

fire engine

Ship Shape

To parents

On this page, your child will paste a triangular sticker. The corners are smaller than right angles, so it is more difficult for young children to align the edges. Your child will gradually learn to paste more accurately, so do not worry if he or she can't do it right away.

Paste the sticker onto the ship.

ship

Big Dig

To parents

On this page, there is only one way to paste the sticker onto the white space. If your child is having difficulty, please help him or her find the correct orientation.

Paste the sticker onto the backhoe.

backhoe

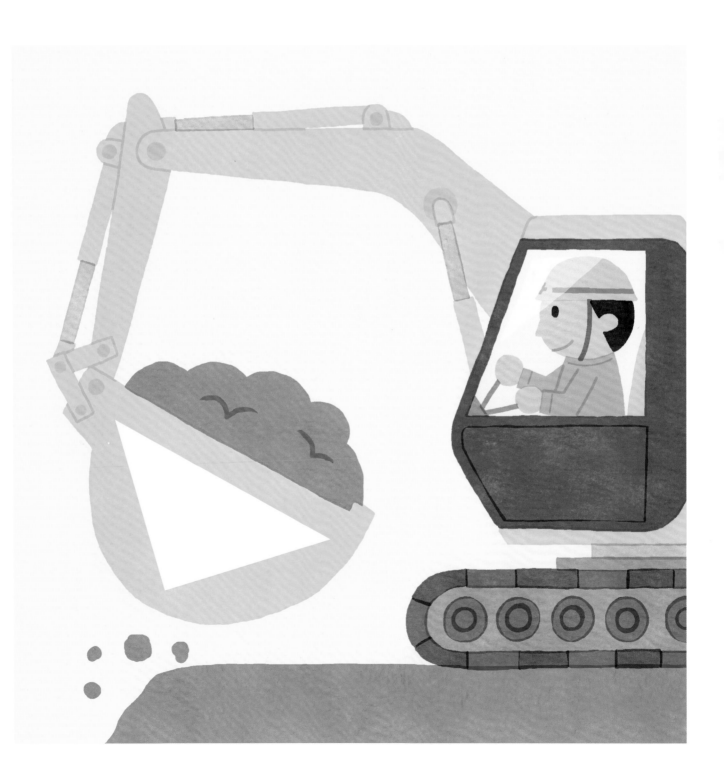

 **Jet Journey**

 Done!

To parents

On this page, there are two stickers to paste. It is not easy for young children to pick the sticker that has the same shape as the white space and the same color as the surrounding area. If your child is having difficulty, please assist him or her by giving a hint like, "Which white space is the square?"

Paste the stickers onto the jet plane.

jet plane

14 Helicopter Up High

Paste the stickers onto the helicopter.

helicopter

 **Cop Car**

To parents

Until now, your child has pasted stickers that do not have patterns or designs. Don't be concerned if your child does not paste the sticker perfectly on this page. If he or she is aware that the black side should be on the bottom, please offer lots of praise.

Paste the sticker onto the police car.

police car

Stickers ①

To be used in ①

To be used in ②

To be used in ③

TAXI

Stickers ❷

To be used in 4

To be used in 5

To be used in 6

 # 16 Hear the Siren?

 Done!

To parents

Your child will paste a circular sticker and a sticker shaped like a passenger window. When your child has finished the activity, talk with him or her about the picture. You can say something like, "Ambulances take sick or injured people to hospitals. Do you know what an ambulance sounds like?" and make the sound of a siren.

Paste the stickers onto the ambulance.

ambulance

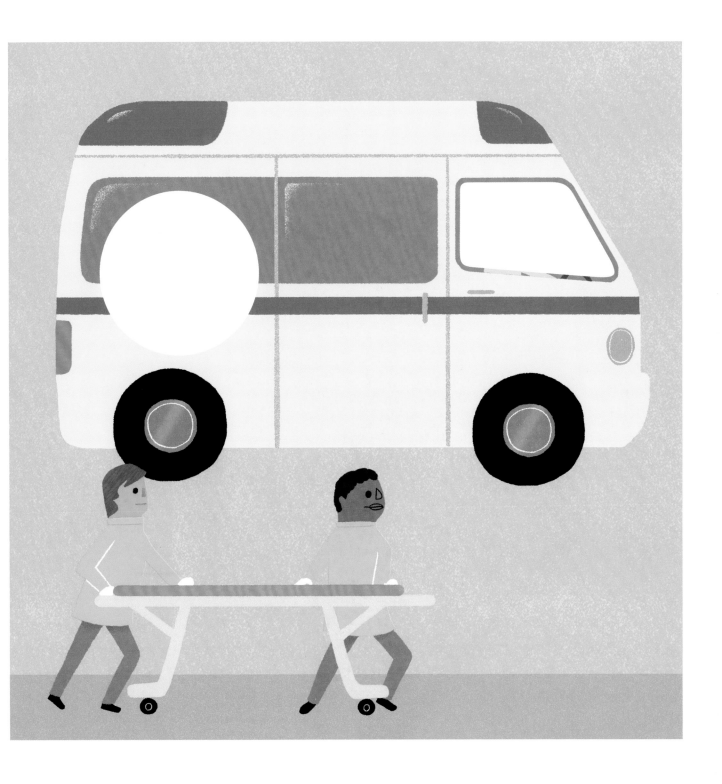

 **Train Trip**

To parents

Please remove the fourth sheet of stickers and give it to your child. (This sheet of stickers is for exercises 17 through 23.) The designs on each sticker are complicated, so don't worry if your child does not paste each sticker perfectly. This activity will be more fun if you talk with your child about seeing or taking a real train.

Paste the stickers onto the train.

train

 **Tour on a Train**

Paste the stickers onto the regional train.

regional train

19 A Visitor Arrives

To parents

There is a square sticker and a circular sticker for this page. Your child can paste each sticker in many different ways, but there is only one correct orientation to complete the illustration of the high-speed train. If your child is aware of matching the illustration, please offer lots of praise.

Paste the stickers onto the high-speed train.

high-speed train

Double-Decker Drive

To parents
The colors and designs on each sticker are similar, so it may be difficult for your child to choose the correct one. Please offer a hint if your child is having difficulty. When he or she has finished the activity, please offer lots of praise.

Paste the stickers onto the double-decker bus.

double-decker bus

Taking a Taxi

To parents

It is difficult for young children to match the edges of stickers perfectly to the white space. Your child will gradually learn to paste accurately, so do not worry if he or she cannot do it right away.

Paste the stickers onto the taxi.

taxi

 **Loco for Locomotives**

To parents

This is the last page where your child will match the designs on the stickers to the background. The design on the locomotive is very intricate, so it may be difficult for your child to complete this page. Please offer lots of praise even if your child can't match the illustration perfectly.

Paste the stickers onto the locomotive.

locomotive

 # Caution at the Crossing

To parents

From this page on, your child will paste stickers to complete parts of the vehicles or scenes. It will be more fun if you talk with your child about each vehicle or memories of a time you spent in a vehicle together.

Paste the stickers to complete the scene.

railroad crossing

 **Biking Adventure**

To parents

Please remove the fifth sheet of stickers and give it to your child. (This sheet of stickers is for exercises 24 through 26.) The sticker of the child has a complicated shape, so it is more difficult to match the white space. When your child has finished the activity, say "bicycle" aloud while pointing to the word.

Paste the stickers to complete the scene.

bicycle

 # In the Driver's Seat

To parents

If your child has not seen a driver's seat many times, this exercise will be challenging. If your child is having trouble finding the place for each sticker, you can lead him or her by pointing out the correct space. If your child loves cars, you both can pretend to drive after the activity is finished.

Paste the stickers to complete the scene.

driver's seat

Time at the Train Station

To parents

On this page, your child will paste train cars and a shop to complete the train station platform. It will be more fun if you talk with your child about a time that you were both on a train station platform watching trains and passengers.

Paste the stickers to complete the scene.

train station

Crossing the Crosswalk

To parents

Please remove the sixth sheet of stickers and give it to your child. (This sheet of stickers is for exercises 27 through 30.) This page includes some small stickers, so please tell your child to sticker with care.

Paste the stickers to complete the scene.

crosswalk

 **Hauling Heavy Cars**

To parents

A car hauler is a kind of truck that carries automobiles. Your child can paste four cars onto the trailer. It does not matter if the image that your child creates isn't like the example. You can ask, "Have you ever seen a truck like this?" and have fun.

Paste the stickers to complete the scene.

car hauler

29 Ride the Rollercoaster

Example

Paste the stickers to complete the scene.

rollercoaster

30 Returning Home

To parents

This is the last exercise in this workbook. Compare your child's work on this exercise with his or her earlier work. You will probably notice a lot of progress in your child's motor control skills. Offer lots of praise along with the Certificate of Achievement on the next page.

Paste the stickers to complete the scene.

garage

Certificate of Achievement

_____

is hereby congratulated on completing

Step-by-Step Stickers: Trains, Planes, and More

Good job!

Presented on _____, 20 ___

_____
Parent or Guardian